0 0001 6084054 2

MAIN
MAR 2000

P9-DBI-790

IRON JOHN

MARIANNA MAYER
WINSLOW PELS

MORROW JUNIOR BOOKS
NEW YORK

For TT
who has cleared a secret path into
the wildwood for me to follow
—M.M.

For my wise
(and often merry) Anna,
and for favorite wild men
Josh, Alex, Lucas, and Wyatt
—W.P.

Pencil, casein, and egg tempera
were used for the full-color illustrations.
The text type is 12-point Hiroshige.

Text copyright © 1999 by Marianna Mayer
Illustrations copyright © 1999 by Winslow Pels

All rights reserved. No part of this book may be reproduced or
utilized in any form or by any means, electronic or mechanical,
including photocopying, recording, or by any information storage and
retrieval system, without permission in writing from the Publisher.

Published by Morrow Junior Books
a division of William Morrow and Company, Inc.
1350 Avenue of the Americas, New York, NY 10019
www.williammorrow.com

Printed in Singapore at Tien Wah Press.

1 2 3 4 5 6 7 8 9 10

Library of Congress Cataloging-in-Publication Data
Mayer, Marianna.
Iron John/as told by Marianna Mayer; illustrated by Winslow Pels.
p. cm.
Summary: With the help of Iron John, also known as the wild man of the forest,
a young prince makes his way in the world and finds his true love.
ISBN 0-688-11554-3 (trade)—ISBN 0-688-11555-1 (library)
[1. Fairy tales.   2. Folklore—Germany.]   I. Pels, Winslow, ill.   II. Title.
PZ8.M4514Ir 1999   398.2'0943'02—dc21   [E]   97-45664   CIP   AC

In days of old, the great magician
Merlin traveled the land, taking on
many guises to test promising young
knights. Sometimes he was an old man or
not a man at all but an animal—a stag
perhaps, or a dragon. And then sometimes,
I am told, he took the form of a Wild Man—
a creature both man and beast, who lived
among the animals in the woodland as
their protector.

 NE RAINY MORNING A SMALL
GRAY BIRD FLEW HEEDLESS OF HER
DIRECTION, SO ANXIOUS WAS SHE TO
escape a hunter's arrows. The arrows fell short of
the mark as the small bird flew on and on until at
last she reached an enchanted wood. There not
a creature stirred. The trees were bare of leaves
and the sun was veiled in clouds. At the heart of
the wood lay a still pond, and beneath its glassy
surface lived John, master of the wood.

Exhausted, the bird came to rest upon a
branch just above the pond. The instant she
alighted, her slight figure vanished.

It was John's magic at work, for he cast a
mantle of invisibility over all the wild creatures
who sought refuge in the wood. And, though
hunters saw the best game disappear into that
dismal forest, only the uninformed stepped
willingly into this protected domain. Fearful
rumors kept out all others. "Hunt there," it was
said, "and it will be *you* who is hunted." Though
no one could say for certain, it was believed a
Wild Man lived deep in the wood, and it was
he who was blamed.

HANS, THE YOUNG PRINCE OF THE FAMILY WHOSE LAND BORDERED THE WOOD, WAS FASCINATED BY THE STORIES. HIS OLD NURSE TOLD HIM TALES OF THE WILD Man, sometimes threatening the prince when he was naughty by saying, "The Wild Man will come and eat you up." Hans didn't believe her warning for a moment, but he would at last take his medicine or go to bed or stop whatever it was he shouldn't do, just to please her.

What Hans did believe were those tales in which the Wild Man had once been a warrior king as well as an enchanter. In fact, such tales were true. Yet for reasons known only to himself, the Wild Man had left his kingdom for the wood where now he ruled as guardian. But alas, there are consequences to such profound protection, for the forest ceased to grow and now stood frozen in time. Nothing bad could happen there, but neither could anything good.

One day a giant of a man covered from head to toe in the skins of animals came to the royal castle, claiming to be the greatest trapper in the land. When the king invited him to supper, the man grinned, revealing a set of rotten teeth, and announced, "I've heard rumors of a Wild Man." He winked a cold black eye at young Hans, playing nearby. "I'll rid you of him, Your Highness," he boasted. "All I ask is three bags of gold."

HE KING GLADLY AGREED, SUPPOSING
HE HAD NOTHING TO LOSE.

WITH HIS SKINNY YELLOW HUNTING
dog close at his heels, the trapper walked into
the gloomy forest. It wasn't long before the dog
ran on ahead and began to bark incessantly
at the edge of a still pond. The trapper came
running and arrived just in time to see a large
shaggy hand the color of rusty iron reach out
of the pond for the dog.

T HE TERRIFIED TRAPPER TURNED BACK
TO THE CASTLE FOR HELP AND QUICKLY
ORDERED THE MEN THERE TO HURRY
and follow him. Using buckets, they emptied
the pond of its water. At the very bottom they
found the Wild Man.

Before he could fight them off with his
magic, the men threw iron chains over him, for
iron was said to render a magician powerless.
Indeed, when they dragged him before the king,
the Wild Man had barely enough strength to lift
his head and face his captors.

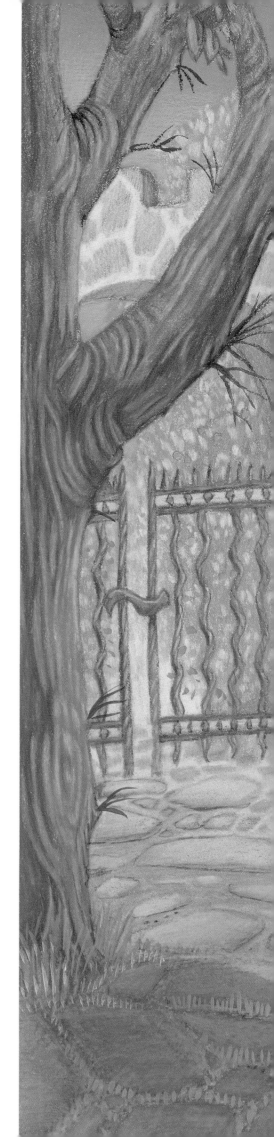

THE PRISONER CAUSED A STIR AMONG THE
NOBLES AND PEASANTS: THEY LAUGHED
AT HIM AND CALLED HIM IRON JOHN
because of his chains and rusty color. The king
had Iron John locked up in a cage in the open
courtyard for all to see. The queen was entrusted
with the key, and the king declared that no one
need fear the wildwood any longer.

At first people flocked to view the caged man.
But since he did nothing more than sit silently
day and night with his eyes cast down, they soon
grew bored—all except Hans, whose interest only
grew. Every day he played quietly with his ball
beside the iron cage.

One morning the ball bounced in. "Will you
give me my ball?" asked Hans.

"No," answered Iron John. "Not unless you
unlock the cage."

"I can't," replied Hans. "The king has
forbidden it."

THE NEXT DAY THE KING AND QUEEN WERE AWAY, AND HANS WAS LEFT ALONE. HE RETURNED TO IRON JOHN and said, "Even if I wanted to unlock the cage, I couldn't, for I don't have the key."

"It is under your mother's pillow," said Iron John, for there was little he did not know.

Hans wanted his ball, but he also hated seeing the Wild Man caged. So he went to the queen's chamber and brought back the key. The rusty lock was hard to force, and he pinched his finger so severely it bled. At last the lock gave, the door creaked open, and Iron John stepped out.

Handing the boy the ball, Iron John turned to leave. But Hans cried, "You must take me with you. If you don't, I'll be beaten for setting you free."

IRON JOHN PAUSED AND CONSIDERED THE TEARFUL CHILD. FINALLY HE PICKED HIM UP, PLACED HIM UPON HIS BROAD SHOULDERS, AND ran from the castle straight for the wildwood.

Soon everything Hans knew was far, far away and a glittering sylvan world lay before him. No animals ran to hide—and there were many, for though they were invisible to others, Hans could see them because he was with Iron John. "Welcome to my kingdom," said Iron John as he and the child went still deeper into the wood. "Here all creatures are treated as equals and need not fear the hunters' arrows."

That first night, when Hans and Iron John reached the deepest, darkest part of the wood, they came to rest. "Your old life is behind you now," said Iron John. "But I will be your second father and teach you the ways of the wild so that you will always love and respect it. I have great riches and power—more than you can imagine. From now on I will protect you, for I am grateful that you gave me back my freedom."

Iron John made Hans a bed of sweet-smelling pine needles and then began a tale of the wildwood, and in no time the small boy fell fast asleep.

THE NEXT MORNING IRON JOHN TOOK HANS TO A STREAM THAT FLOWED INTO A LARGE POND. "THIS IS A MAGIC STREAM. YOUR TASK WILL BE TO PROTECT IT. MAKE SURE NOTHING FALLS INTO ITS WATERS. EACH NIGHT I'll come to see if you have guarded it well."

All day Hans sat beside the stream. He watched small golden fish and a thin golden snake glide by. He took care that nothing fell into the water.

Then, as the sun began to set, the finger he had pinched in the lock began to burn. Without thinking, he plunged it into the cool water. Only then did Hans remember that *nothing* was to enter the stream. He quickly pulled his finger out, but it had turned gold!

That evening Iron John returned and asked, "Did you put anything in the water?"

Too frightened to answer, Hans held his finger behind his back.

Iron John frowned. "You put your finger into the stream. You must keep to your task. If you fail, I will have to send you away."

Early the next morning the boy's finger began to burn again. This time he rubbed it against the side of his head and a strand of his hair fell into the water. He pulled it out, but it too had turned gold.

When Iron John returned, he knew what had happened and said, "I will forgive this second mistake, my son. But if you fail a third time, you will have to leave me."

On the third day, no matter how much his finger hurt, Hans did nothing. But as the hours passed, he grew bored and began to gaze at his own reflection mirrored on the water's surface. Closer and closer he leaned until he was so near that his hair fell into the stream. He pulled his head up quickly, but his hair had already turned gold.

I N DESPAIR HANS PUT ON HIS CAP AND TUCKED HIS HAIR INSIDE. IT WAS NO USE. WHEN IRON JOHN RETURNED, HE SAID, "TAKE OFF YOUR CAP."

HANS OBEYED, AND HIS NOW BEAUTIFUL GOLDEN HAIR TUMBLED DOWN to his shoulders. "Though it saddens me, I must send you away," said Iron John. "But I will never forget you. If you need help, come into the wood and call me. Wherever I am, I will come to your aid."

That very night Hans journeyed out of the wildwood. By morning he had passed beyond the last stand of ancient pines that separated the enchanted wood from the rest of the world. Here Hans stopped beside a river to quench his thirst. As he drank, he saw to his astonishment that he was a child no longer, but a young man grown tall and strong. It seemed that he had been with Iron John only a few days, but in fact many years had passed while

he was in that enchanted wood.

Hans never forgot Iron John, and as he went in search of work, he took care to help creatures in need. Once he came upon a man beating a donkey. The animal was old and could no longer pull the burdens the man demanded. Hans bought the donkey with the few coins he had earned from hard labor. In the same way he rescued a lame dog he saw cruelly mistreated by a group of heartless boys.

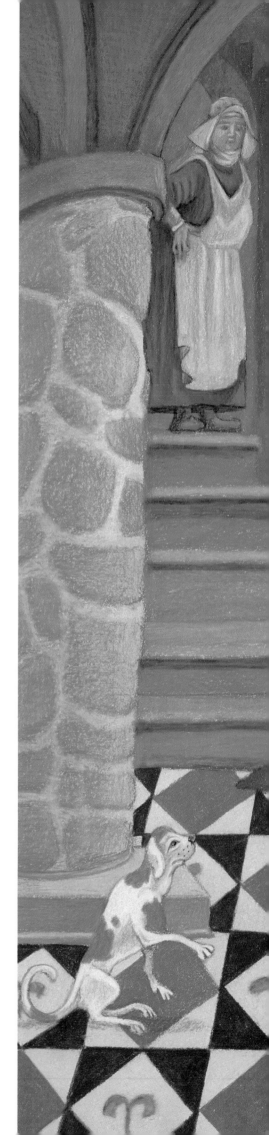

INALLY ONE DAY HANS FOUND HIS WAY TO A PALACE IN A GREAT CITY. THE GATEKEEPER PITIED THE YOUNG MAN STANDING BEFORE him with the old donkey and the lame dog. He sent Hans to the palace cook, who gave him work and shelter for his animals.

 From then on Hans fetched water and wood for the cook's kitchen. One day he had to carry the breakfast tray to the king and his daughter. "When you serve at the

royal table, you must remove your cap," remarked the king as Hans set down the tray, still wearing the cap he always wore to conceal his bright golden hair.

"But Your Majesty," Hans answered, "I cannot."

The princess covered her mouth to hide her smile at his bold reply, but the king was annoyed. He sent word to the cook to have Hans dismissed. Instead the cook found Hans work with the master gardener.

ONE SUMMER AFTERNOON IT WAS SO HOT IN THE
GARDEN THAT HANS REMOVED HIS CAP TO WIPE
HIS BROW. HIS GOLDEN HAIR FELL DOWN TO HIS
shoulders. It was still as bright as sunshine itself.

The princess, gazing out her window, couldn't help but
notice him. Wishing to get a better look at the handsome
young man, she called, "Gardener, gather a bouquet of
flowers and bring it to me."

Hans picked carefully, for from the first
he thought the princess the most wonderful
girl he had ever seen. He gathered wild
daisies, lilies, roses, and yarrow. Tenderly
he tied them together and carried them to
the princess's chamber.

"Why, you've brought me wildflowers," remarked the
princess, delighted.

"They are my favorite," said Hans, too shy to meet
her eyes.

"You are the same young man who once
refused to remove your cap," observed the
princess. Hans nodded. "Will you remove it
now?" she asked.

"I cannot," Hans replied.

Impulsively the princess snatched it off.

Out tumbled his shimmering hair. But the princess, seeing his
embarrassment, regretted her boldness. Before he could dash
away, she pressed a gold coin into his hand and quietly asked
his pardon.

The princess couldn't stop thinking
about the puzzling young gardener. Each
day she called for a fresh bouquet and
each day she gave Hans another gold coin
for his trouble. Though Hans accepted the
coins, the princess later learned from the master gardener that
Hans had given them all to the gardener's children. This news
left her more puzzled than before.

NOT LONG AFTER, AN ENEMY'S ARMY ATTACKED THE KINGDOM. THE INVADERS' VICTORY SEEMED ASSURED, FOR THE KING'S TROOPS WERE FAR OUTNUMBERED. Hans was quick to volunteer, for by now he was in love with the princess, and though he felt sure she could never love him, he wished to do his part to protect her.

But the captain of the guard only mocked him. "What does a gardener know of battle?" As a joke he sent Hans to the stable, but there were no warhorses left, only Hans's old donkey.

Undaunted, Hans led the animal out of the stable and disappeared into the dark wood. Reaching a clearing, he called out, *Iron John!* His voice echoed through the forest.

The next moment the Wild Man stood before him. "It's been a long time, my son. What do you need?"

"I wish to go into battle, but I am without a strong horse to ride."

"You shall have one, and more," replied Iron John. All at once a groom appeared, leading a magnificent warhorse. His shiny black hooves pounded the ground; he reared and arched his powerful neck. Then a mighty host of soldiers clad in gleaming armor came riding into the clearing.

ANS MOUNTED THE STEED AND, LEADING HIS NEW ARMY, RODE INTO BATTLE. MANY OF THE KING'S MEN HAD FALLEN ON THE BATTLEFIELD, WHILE THE REST were making a hasty retreat. The swords of his troops were blazing as Hans gave orders to advance. Like a sudden storm he took command of the field and quickly defeated the enemy. Full of praise for the surprising victory, the king summoned the unknown hero. But Hans turned away and rode off with his troops.

Back in the wildwood, he returned the fine warhorse and armored soldiers to Iron John with his thanks. As Hans led the old donkey away, Iron John stopped him. "Why," he asked, "did you not claim your rightful reward from the king?"

Hans shook his head. "He would not have been pleased to learn that his kingdom was saved by a gardener. In any case, the victory was yours."

"You are too modest, my son," replied Iron John. "I provided the horse and troops, but your skill and courage won the battle."

Of course everyone wanted to know who the mysterious champion was. The princess had her own suspicions, although she could not say why. Privately she asked the master gardener where Hans had been during the battle. "I doubt he ever made it to the field, for he had to ride his old donkey," explained the man. So it was not the young gardener after all, thought the princess, and yet something told her there was more to him than anyone knew.

T HE KING, MEANWHILE, WAS DETERMINED TO FIND OUT WHO HIS DELIVERER WAS. TO HIS DAUGHTER HE CONFIDED, "TOMORROW I SHALL HOLD A VICTORY celebration with a tournament of games for every knight to test his skills. At the end of the games, you will throw the grand prize—a golden apple. The knight who catches it will be named the champion. I am sure our elusive hero will be unable to resist the temptation to compete, and this time he will not get away so easily."

As soon as the tournament was announced, Hans returned to Iron John. "What can I do for you, my son?" Iron John asked.

"I want to compete at the king's tournament, but I must have armor and a horse."

"I will help you," answered Iron John.

The next day Hans joined the other knights at the games, wearing Iron John's gift of flame red armor and riding a handsome chestnut stallion. No one knew who he was, though to the amazement of the crowd and the great frustration of the other knights, this brilliant stranger won game after game. As the day wore on, tension built— until finally the princess stepped forward, holding the

golden apple. Anxiously the crowd waited, hoping for the red knight to claim this last victory so his identity would be revealed.

Armor clanged and nervous horses snorted and pranced as the knights roughly jostled one another for position. At last there was silence. All eyes were on the gleaming golden apple as the princess threw it into the air. Soaring overhead, the prize seemed for an instant suspended in midair. And then, just at that moment, the red knight reached out and caught the apple in his outstretched hand.

C HEERING FOR THE RED KNIGHT'S TRIUMPH, THE CROWD BURST THROUGH THE TOURNAMENT barriers and rushed to surround him. But Hans turned and galloped away. Expecting as much, the king signaled his men to follow. "There will be a grand reward for the one who brings him back!" he promised.

The other knights set out in pursuit, only too eager to catch this knight who had bested them all. Finally one rode close enough to try to pull Hans's horse down. In the struggle, his helmet fell to the ground, uncovering his striking golden hair.

Determined not to be caught, Hans spurred his horse on, but his escape was blocked by a thick bank of tall bushes. He was trapped and his pursuers closed in, but then the chestnut steed made a stunning leap and cleared the bushes. The other horses refused the jump, leaving their riders looking on helplessly as Hans disappeared.

O N HEARING THE DETAILS OF THE CHASE, THE PRINCESS MADE UP HER MIND TO HAVE THE YOUNG GARDENER SUMMONED BEFORE THE KING. WHEN Hans arrived, she surprised him by reaching for his cap. Too late, he stepped back and out tumbled his glorious golden hair for all to see.

"You are the knight who rode off with the golden apple!" said the king.

"Yes," admitted Hans, and taking the golden apple from his pocket, he placed it before the king.

"And you are also the champion who saved our kingdom."

"Yes," Hans replied reluctantly.

"Tell us more—for certainly you're not simply a gardener."

"Once I was the son of a king of a distant land, but that was long ago," Hans began. "But my adopted father, who lives in the wildwood, raised me. It is he who has helped me. Without him I would not have become the man I am today."

"You deserve a great reward for what you have done for us," insisted the king. "Ask what you will, and I shall grant it."

"Riches mean little to me, Your Majesty," replied Hans. "I ask only that the wild lands surrounding your castle be given over to me, so that I might live the rest of my life there."

"Consider it done," said the king. "But is there *nothing* else you wish?"

"Aye, Sire," said Hans with a wry smile, "I wish for your daughter's love, but this cannot be given as a prize. It is hers to give freely or not at all."

The princess, whose name was Terre, at first had been disappointed when Hans had not asked for her hand in marriage. Now she was surprised and touched by his words.

"I am a woman who knows her own mind," she replied. "And as you are a man who knows his, you have won my love without asking." And she went to him and kissed him.

S OON A WEDDING WAS CELEBRATED, AND
AS THE SINGING AND FEASTING WENT ON,
SUDDENLY THE DOORS TO THE ROYAL HALL
burst open. All heads turned as a tall, regally
dressed man entered, followed by a host of
attendants. The unknown king went to Hans.

"Do you remember me?"
he asked.

"You are Iron John, my
second father," said Hans.
"Richly robed or not, I
would know you."

Iron John smiled and
said, "Long ago I turned away from the world,
preferring the company of wild creatures in
the refuge I made in the wood. My heart had
hardened toward humankind for their greed and
cruelty. But you, Hans, remind me that there is
also goodness in the human soul. When you
spoke of the gifts I gave you, you did not
consider the gift that you yourself have been to
me. I name you heir to all my wealth and power,
knowing you will use them both wisely."

H ANS AND TERRE LIVED OUT THEIR LIVES
IN THE LUSH GREEN WOODLAND. THERE
THEY BUILT A HANDSOME SHELTER FROM
which every view of the wildwood was a picture
beyond compare. As the years passed, they had
many children, who grew up knowing the
priceless beauty of such a life.

And those fortunate enough to know the place
where this good family dwelt could say with
conviction that it was indeed a paradise on earth.

ABOUT THIS STORY

The myth of a noble wild man, living in the wilderness with the animals he has befriended, dates back to ancient history. Descriptions of him can be traced to 2000 B.C. in the Babylonian hero epic *Gilgamesh* and to an even earlier Sumerian tale of the same name. Tales of wild men have been recorded from the twelfth century into the twentieth century, including Geoffrey of Monmouth's *Vita Merlini.* This twelfth-century retelling of a sixth-century event portrays the legendary Merlin as a prophet and wild man. In fact, both Merlin and Iron John can be compared to the ancient Celtic stag-god, Cernunnos, who lived alone in the wildwood, possessed supernatural powers, and had under his protection all the beasts in the forest.

While the wild man has remained with us over time, his image has undergone considerable transformation. Once thought of as a pagan deity, today he is romanticized in films such as *Tarzan* and in books such as *Iron John,* a work of popular psychology written by poet Robert Bly. The wild man is also central to our contemporary legends of Bigfoot, the Abominable Snowman, and other speculations about the existence of the missing link between primitive and modern humankind.

What enthralls us about the noble savage, who possesses human intelligence as well as animal passion and instincts? Perhaps such wild creatures are perceived as freer than ourselves, able to live at one with the natural world. With scientists and environmentalists warning that our wildlife is in peril, it seems significant that a more reverent image of the wild man should again enter the popular consciousness. Perhaps we are looking to be reminded that we must be responsible stewards of the earth in order to share its bounty with countless other creatures. In my own adaptation of the wild man myth, I have sought to convey the truth Iron John learned and shared with Hans.

BIBLIOGRAPHICAL NOTE

A number of sources were key in constructing my version of this story—*Der Eisenhans,* collected from the nineteenth-century German oral tradition by the Brothers Grimm; *Vita Merlini,* by Geoffrey of Monmouth, edited by J. S. Tatlock; *The Adventures of Suibne Geilt, a Middle-Irish Romance,* edited and translated by J. G. O'Keeffe; *Yvain* and *Perceval,* by Chrétien de Troyes; *The King and the Corpse: Tales of the Soul's Conquest of Evil,* by Heinrich Zimmer; *Legend of Lailoken: Wild Men in the Middle Ages,* by Richard Bernheimer; *The Wild Man Within: An Image in Western Thought from the Renaissance to Romanticism,* edited by Edward J. Dudley and Maximillian E. Novak; and *Green Man: The Archetype of Our Oneness with the Earth,* by William Anderson.